MY MISADVENTURES AS A TEENAGE ROCK STAR

MY MISADVENTURES AS A TEENAGE ROCK STAR

WRITTEN BY JOYCE RASKIN
ILLUSTRATIONS BY CAROL CHU

Houghton Mifflin Harcourt
Boston New York 2011

Text copyright © 2011 by Joyce Raskin
Illustrations copyright © 2011 by Carol Chu

For information about permission to reproduce selections from this book,
write to Permissions, Houghton Mifflin Harcourt Publishing Company,
215 Park Avenue South, New York, New York 10003.

Graphia and the Graphia logo are registered
trademarks of Houghton Mifflin Harcourt
Publishing Company.

www.hmhbooks.com

The text of this book is set in Adobe Garamond.
Book design by Carol Chu

Library of Congress Cataloging-in-Publication Data

Raskin, Joyce.
My misadventures as a teenage rock star / by Joyce Raskin ;
[illustrated by] Carol Chu. p. cm.
Summary: Fourteen-year-old Alex, a short, pasty, shy, greasy-haired girl
with acne, gains self-confidence when her brother convinces her to play
bass in a rock band, but she finds that being "cool" has its drawbacks.
ISBN 978-0-547-39311-7
[1. Self-confidence—Fiction. 2. Popularity—Fiction.
3. Bands (Music)—Fiction. 4. Rock music—Fiction.
5. Family life—New Jersey—Fiction. 6. New Jersey—Fiction.]
I. Chu, Carol, ill. II. Title.
PZ7.R18182Mis 2011
[Fic]—dc22   2010027456

Manufactured in China
LEO 10 9 8 7 6 5 4 3 2 1

4500281683

Hello, My Name Is Alex

1

Hello, my name is Alex. I'm fourteen years old. I'm a rock star. My book is all about what it's like being a rock star, a teenager, and a girl— all at the same time (which is *a lot*). Being fourteen is hard, but playing music helps me through all the tough times.

I wasn't always a rock star. Before I turned fourteen, here's what my life was like . . .

(Flashback begins. Hum flashback-type music here in your mind. *Di di di di di di di*).

We have been transported to the room of a young teenager in a typical house in the suburbs of New Jersey. The girl sits in front of her pink unicorn mirror gazing at her reflection. This is Alex, short for Alexis. She's a short, pasty, shy, greasy-haired kid with a face full of acne. The kids in her middle school call her Zit Fit. She looks like she's ten. Her biggest obsession is comparing herself with models and movie stars.

Not very healthy; guess that's why it's called it an obsession.

Alex struggles with many different hairstyles as she tries to make herself look pretty.

A side ponytail, just like that teen pop star Haley. Yes? No.

Perhaps the cheerleader ponytail? Not!

A big barrette. Now she looks like she's eight. This is so not working.

Alex messes her hair up and shrieks, *"Ahhhhh!"*

Her mother shouts, "Everything all right in there, Alexis?"

"Yes," Alex shouts back. "No," she mumbles to herself. "Everything is definitely not all right."

Alex *must, must, must* learn how to make herself pretty! Even her name isn't pretty. Alexis. Yuck. A boy's name for sure. What were her parents thinking when

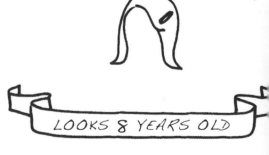

they named her Alexis, AKA Alex? Were they hoping for a boy? Maybe they suddenly experienced some mental confusion after her birth and forgot they had a daughter? It's possible. As her parents are pretty nice people, they would never stick her with an ugly name on purpose.

Alex's mom is kind of a hippy and really into yoga and meditating and all that stuff. She often tells Alex that she needs to get in touch with her inner self to find her inner beauty.

Alex attempts the following things to find her so-called inner beauty:

1. Alex begins writing in her diary all her inner thoughts. *I am a nice person. I am a good person. I am an okay person. I am a sad person because I have no friends. I am a loser because I am so ugly. I am ugly, ugly,*

ugly. Why am I so ugly? Ugly, ugly, ugly, UGLY, UGLY. She gets stuck on rewriting the word *ugly* all the way down the page with curly flower decorations on the letters. She throws the diary onto the floor and begins sobbing hysterically.

2. Once the tears dry and she's in a state of quiet calm, Alex tries meditation to unload her chakras. She begins with the *Om*s while sitting in the lotus position. Eventually the *Om*s turn into this chant:

"*Om,* I hate pretty girls, *Om,* who are blond with cute button noses. *Om,* I want to be them. *Om,* why was I born this way? *Om,* help me, please! *Om,* someone? *Om,* anyone, *oh,* listening? *Oh, Aghhh, Oh, uh,* the silence is killing me. *Om,* and this position is, too. *Ugh.*"

3. Alex gets up and shakes out her legs. She walks over to a pile of magazines on the floor and picks out one with a blond girl in a bikini on the cover. She begins flipping through the pages until she finds the advice section. As she sits down at her pink desk and picks up a pink and purple feather pen, her

face is filled with intense concentration as she begins to write a letter to the magazine. She writes, "Dear TeenHelper, I'm in need of help," then rips it up. She starts again. And again and again. Every letter ends up crumpled in the rainbow wastebasket next to the desk. She finally abandons this futile project and flops onto her bed with a sigh. Another magazine cover catches her eye and lifts her momentarily out of her misery. A brunette girl wearing a shimmery dress under the headline "An Outfit to Make You Cool" gives Alex an idea.

4. Alex convinces her mother to drive her to the mall. Wearing her best purple and pink matching outfit with a T-shirt that says UNICORNS ARE COOL, Alex feels like she has found a solution to all her problems. As she passes a group of blond girls they laugh at her, and she lowers her head. She enters the big department store and collects all the pieces of an outfit, then finds out her allowance will only pay for the headband.

She walks past the group of laughing girls a second time, only now she's carrying a small plastic bag with the headband inside. *Pathetic.*

Now Alex is back in her room, where she sits with tears in her eyes. She's staring once again at her reflection in the mirror and saying out loud, "I must think of a way to get enough money for plastic surgery to transform me into a model. It's the only way to make me pretty. Or I need my Fairy Godmother to appear. Fairy Godmother, where are you? This is your chance—I need you!"

After her Fairy Godmother fails to appear, Alex picks up her diary again and begins writing down some notes. She then proceeds to read them to the mirror. "Here is my list of requirements for being a pretty girl. If you are listening, Fairy Godmother, this is what I need:

1. Long blond hair (Could consider hair dye, but what about my eyebrows? Is there a manual for this stuff? Must check the library—they have books on everything!)

2. Hip, trendy clothes (These cost more money than my allowance.)

3. A taller, thinner body (I would wear high heels if I weren't such a klutz.)

4. Nice boobs (I barely have any at all. Maybe when I get my period they will grow some more?)

5. A good name like Jenny, Sarah, or Lily (Must investigate changing my name legally.)

6. A boyfriend (Working on it.)

7. Nice lips to kiss with (Working on it.)

8. Lots of friends (Working on it.)

9. Look like you are having fun all the time (Working on it.)

Alex begins sobbing. "Fairy Godmother, where are you? Fairy

Godmother, where are you! Damn you, Fairy Godmother! I'm definitely not going to believe in you anymore! Thank god for unicorns!" She runs over to her bed and hugs her collection of stuffed unicorns.

(Flash forward. More wavy lines. Hum again, please. *Di di di di di di di di.*)

Then rock-and-roll came into my life, and I was transformed. Maybe something like this will happen to you. Here's what happened to me.

I He_nart "Tod the Mod

STORY #1

My older brother, Charles, has a friend named Tod, also known as Tod the Mod. He's my secret love. He's dating a girl who looks like a model. Her name is Jenny (*of course*). Perhaps only pretty people can have pretty names? I have a boy's name. Go figure.

Tod's in a band. He plays keyboards and the drum machine. He has a leather jacket. He has spiky blond hair and green eyes. Tod listens to weird music no one else has ever heard of. *He* is cool. He's dreamy like a movie star. I hate Jenny. She gets to kiss Tod.

One Saturday, Tod and Charles are sitting in the basement of our house talking about bands and listening to music, and they invite me to come down and hang out with them. I guess my sitting at the top of the stairs, eavesdropping, kind of gave them a hint that was what I wanted to do. So I sit down next to Tod on the plaid couch.

I feel kind of lost when they talk about things like "riffs, grooves, and the beat." I wish I knew what they were talking about. But at least I'm hanging out with Tod, and *anything* out of Tod's mouth sounds wonderful.

Then I start to daydream (something I'm really good at) while they are talking. I imagine I have magically been transformed into Jenny. *Tod and I are in some romantic setting, with candles and a view of the ocean* (I'm really good at this, huh?). *Tod turns to me. Tod looks at me. And, just like in the movies, we kiss a long, slow kiss . . .*

And I'm woken when I hear my brother say that *I* could play bass for Tod's band? *What?* And Tod really *is* looking at me. I have shrunk to my former self in an instant.

I start to panic. I start to sweat. I can smell that my deodorant is not working well at all. (I should consider changing brands, as this one does no good under pressure.) I hope that Tod can't smell me.

Ugh, I'm even disgusting myself.

As my mind chatters inside, outside I stare in silence at Tod—just admiring his green eyes, which shimmer so dreamily. He looks like a movie star as he brushes a strand of hair out of his face. I'm distracted momentarily from my stink by Tod's eyes, which are still focused on me. His stare hits me somewhere in my gut, and I'm *fading back into dreamland* . . . I want to melt away, but I'm frozen on the couch by Tod's superpower stare. I'm captured in his superaura of cuteness. It's so strong I cannot even wiggle my toes.

Then *zap!* Charles brings me back to Earth again. I try to recapture my daydream, but all my powers have been diminished by my brother's voice. He can't be in the daydream. *Ick! My brother! Ick! EWW!*

"Well, Alex, what do you think about giving the bass a try? You already know how to play piano. Bass is a cinch compared to that," says Charles.

What do I think? What do I *think? I think you are crazy, Charles!* I scream in my head. I think my brother has lost his mind. Must speak to my mother about this.

Outside I sit like a statue, still afraid to speak or do anything, because once again Tod's looking at me in such a hopeful way. And my daydream powers come back in a flash . . . (Perhaps if I were a superhero, this would be my greatest strength?) Tod opens his kissable lips, and his warm voice asks me the same question. "Yeah, Alex, what do you think? A girl bass player is *really* cool."

The word *cool* drifts off his lips and lands in my general direction in slow-motion heavenliness, and I'm in a movie . . . *I am the pretty movie star, and I am cool.*

"I'll teach you," Charles says matter-of-factly (*Screechhh!* Brother alert! Daydream way over now.)

My brother and Tod are staring at me. Perhaps my daydreaming power suddenly has seeped through the cushions on the couch and up into everyone's mind and given them the same crazy thought: *Alex can be the bass player in Tod's band.*

What would I do with an instrument I know nothing about? lingers somewhere in the back of my mind and then goes away as I look over at Tod again. His sparkling white teeth remind me of a toothbrush ad, and I let out a weak yes.

Tod is my kryptonite. I'm powerless in his gaze.

Tod and Charles both say "cool" in unison. And then they are back in Guy-ville, and I might as well be on Mars. They go back to their conversation about a "mean solo," and reality settles in like a car crash.

What did I just agree to do? I start to panic again, my heart pounding in my ears.

What would a superhero do in this hour of need? *Dun Duh Dah Duh Dah* . . . Daydream Girl to the rescue . . . I think like an intelligent person who knows all (after all, Daydream Girl is a superhero) . . . *Maybe while I was daydreaming I turned into Jenny? Sounds crazy, right? But me playing the bass is even crazier, right?*

I strut down the hallway, walking in slow motion—my beautiful long blond hair flowing behind me, my cool clothes moving freely, showing off my lovely long legs—to the beat of the soundtrack in my head. Cool, cool, cool. Yeah, man, cool. And I look dreamily into the mirror and . . . Not cool at all.

"Oh, still me," I say out loud.

I'm Alex the meek, Alex the loser, and all I can do is start crying. I sit down to pee, still crying (another thing I'm really good at, crying plus anything), and when I get up, there's blood in the toilet and in my underwear. My period has arrived. My life sucks. Most girls are shocked when they get their period. I have been waiting so long, for me it's like winning twelfth place in a contest. At least it stops my crying.

I have one last Daydream Girl thought I muster up from deep down: *Maybe my boobs will now grow? Anything is possible.*

My optimism shocks me. Maybe I was transformed in a small way by daydream power?

Can I Rock?
STORY #2

The next morning at breakfast my brother is still talking to me about playing the bass, and now he even has my parents cheering about Alex their future bass player. Okay, no pressure. Charles reassures me I can do it, no sweat. No sweat? How can my brother not understand me after all these years of living together under the same roof? Nothing I have ever done has been no sweat. Even kindergarten was full of sweat—frustration, embarrassment, anxiousness, and sweat. I wish Charles hadn't decided to wait to get into Brown University, because then he wouldn't be so late to start college and I wouldn't be in this mess. Damn you, Charles.

Charles looks up from his cereal and repeats, "No sweat. See you when you get home from school."

Brothers just don't understand. Why couldn't I have had a sister? But then, if I did and she was prettier than I am, that would suck more than a brother who can't relate to me. I go up to my room to write

a new mantra in my diary to help me get
up the courage to learn the bass guitar. My
new mantra about rock-and-roll: Tod will
think I'm cool if I play bass.

I make a list of everything I know
about the bass and call it my Zen Rock
List. I'm good at making lists: go, List
Girl! Not a superpower possibility, un-
fortunately, but definitely librarian
potential. Good backup plan. Forget
wishing for Fairy Godmothers that
don't exist. I will take care of things
myself from now on. Here's what I
write in my diary:

What I know about the bass guitar:
1. It looks like a guitar.
2. Boys play it to pick up girls.
3. It has four strings.
I shut my diary and run off to catch the bus to school.

After school my brother says it's time for my bass lesson. Doesn't he
have anything better to do than torture me? He really needs to start
college. He's wasting way too much energy on my life.

"Don't you have to get some school supplies or something?" I say.

"Alex, you don't get school supplies in college. I get everything when
I'm up there. Plus, you know Mom. She's already shopped for me, way
more than I need. Now, let's not change the subject. Time to rock,"
Charles says with a laugh.

I feel like I can't do any worse than I did on my math test this
morning. I would like to blame that disaster on my period making me

feel like the grossest person on the planet, but, alas, my math teacher probably wouldn't understand, as he is a guy. Why did I want to get my period so badly? It *sucks*.

BASS LESSON #1

1. Sit bass on your lap.
2. Plug into amp.
3. Makes notes with left hand.
4. Hit the strings with right hand.
5. Cry and suffer through horrible sounds. Cry until my brother says, "Lesson over."

Charles keeps asking me, "Why do girls cry so much? Why do girls cry?" It's futile to explain this to a guy, especially my brother, Mr. No Sweat.

He looks like he might have changed his mind about me playing bass. I don't blame him. I am not a natural. I am dysfunctional in this world of rock-and-roll. Yet, somehow, the next day we are at it again. Perhaps Charles has some hidden sadistic tendencies, but I refrain from mentioning this, as he is trying to be really nice and teach me how to play bass.

BASS LESSON #2

1. You have to land the tip of your left finger exactly between metal bars, or you will only make farting sounds, not notes. *Fart, Fart, Fart.* My bass-playing is full of *farts*. An hour of farting and "lesson over."

My bass-playing stinks. I only make farts. *Not cool!* Will I *ever* have a boyfriend? My fingers are killing me. The tip of every finger is red. Maybe it's my period interfering? *I wish. I do not rock.*

Upon viewing my frustration in full effect after another session of good crying, my hippy mom says, "Be patient. It will come."

Of course, she believes in me. I mean, she is my mom. She *has* to believe in me. It's her job.

BASS LESSON #3

1. I play my first song on the bass, "Let's Go Rock Baby" by a band called the Sedated Messes.
2. I play three notes.
3. I play the song fifty times, farting all the way.
4. I cry every second, and then I get my first . . . *blister!*

The blister is huge. It looks like something out of a science fiction film. It lives on the tip of my finger, mocking my every moment. *Hah! Now you will never, ever get a guy, not with me around! Ahhh! I am hideous!* Why did I decide to do this? My fingers are permanently deformed. I am now more hideous than before, which I didn't think was possible.

My brother's reaction: "So rock-and-roll! You got your first blister! Now you're a *real* bass player."

Daydream Girl rises up in me and says, *Maybe Tod will think so, too?* I will never let this blister pop, even though it's really uncomfortable. *Must make it until Tod can view the blister, and then . . .*

I pop the blister an hour later. The pressure is too much. I can't take it anymore. Water gushes out. *Eww.* I just finished my period, and now this? I will *never* get a boyfriend.

My First Combat Boots
STORY #3

Now that I play bass I think it's
time for me to change my look.
My dad takes me to the army navy-store and
buys me my first pair of combat boots. Eight holes laced
up to the top. Steel toes and black leather. They make me feel tough.
I get my hair cut in an Egyptian-style bob and add a blond streak. I
buy clothes in thrift shops. I have my new, improved look—cool bass-
player chick.

Daydream Girl is now Cool Rock Bass-Player Chick. *Dunt dah dah
dah!* Super Bass Girl to the rescue! I have the power to rock you! *Rock
on!* I've been transformed by rock-and-roll! *Hey, that sounds like a song
title. Maybe I do have a knack for this music stuff?*

At breakfast, Charles laughs at my new look. I want to hit him. He's
the one who made me do all this rock stuff in the first place. He sucks.
I can't wait until he goes to college and butts out of my life. I stare

down at my combat boots and find the courage to feel cool again in my new outfit. I *am* cool, I tell myself. I shake off Charles's comments and do a secret meditation on the bus ride to school. It works, and I'm in supercool rock chick mode again. I strut down the aisle of the bus and feel tough in my combat boots. Some of the preppy kids stare at me in awe. *Yeah, be scared,* I think. I play bass.

Getting off the bus, I feel like I can do anything and I can be anything I want to be. I am on top of the world. I'm cool. I miss the last step off the bus and land face first on the sidewalk at the feet of Stan the skateboarder and all his skater friends. They all start cracking up but thankfully are distracted by the bell. I run as fast as I can into the crowd of kids moving toward the front doors of the school.

I start to feel really stupid again about my new look. Maybe Charles was right to laugh at me. I begin to question everything about my choices so far. What was I thinking? I make it through the rest of the day by sitting in the back of my classes and hiding in a bathroom stall for lunch. My teachers are the only people who seem to notice my elusiveness. But they are adults, so they don't count. I feel thankful for being invisible for once. At last the final bell rings, and I'm ready to run home and dye my hair brown and throw away my combat boots, when Stan the skateboarder comes up to my locker and says, "Dig the blond streak. Are you new at school? This is your first day, huh?"

I decide to go with it, as he is so cute with his shaggy hair, and he's looking at me with his blue eyes. "Yep. Just moved here from Colorado." Pulled that out of nowhere.

"Cool," Stan says. "Wicked snowboarding out there, huh? What's your name?"

"Alex," I say, thinking, *Why didn't I make up a new name, too?*

"Cool, Alex. See ya around," Stan says.

I watch Stan walk down the hall and suddenly feel filled with rock power again. Okay, maybe I will stick with this look a little longer. Stan noticed me. Cool.

The next day I'm very careful getting off the bus, and I see Stan hanging with his friends. I walk by, pretending not to notice, but I can't help but look at him. He waves and skates over to catch up with me.

"Hey, what's up?" Stan says with a smile.

"Nothing," I say, as I really hadn't been up to much. I didn't think my garbage and dish duties or my homework would impress Stan the skateboarder.

"Yesterday we had a blast at the skate park. You should come down and hang with us sometime," Stan says while balancing effortlessly next to me on his board.

"Yeah. Cool," I say, trying to fight the scream of excitement that's building inside me. Don't act goofy. Be Zen, *Om.*

"Later," Stan says, and skates off.

Every day for about three weeks I have a similar encounter with Stan when I get off the bus. Our band, the Painted Letters, started playing a couple of dances and parties, and soon more and more people began to notice the new girl from Colorado. Stan is up front at every show. I feel like my life *is* becoming a movie. Then the most amazing thing happens. Stan the skateboarder calls me on the phone and asks me out

for real. Stan says I'm cute and cool because I
play bass. Stan says he can talk to me—not like
most girls. I can talk about music and bands
with him. That's supercool to Stan. Maybe the
inside *does* count as much as the outside. I enjoy my moment of Zen, with help from my
super bass powers.

 After my moment of Zen (ten minutes
later) I start screaming in my room, "I have a
boyfriend!" I write a song about it on my bass.
I jump around my room singing, "I have a boyfriend, yeah! I have a
boyfriend, *swee-ee-ee-t! Tah! Dunna nanan nah! Uh! Dananan na uh!
Yeah!* I have a boyfriend, and he is mine-oh-mine-ah!" All in the key of
E. The low-E string sounds really rock-and-roll.

 My mom makes me invite Stan over for dinner, and I feel like I
want to die. *Nooooooo!* But my dad insists, as this is my first boyfriend.
We have an awkward dinner, but Stan is so mellow, and even though I
can tell my dad doesn't want me to be with any guy, period, he thinks
Stan is okay. Stan charms my hippy mother.

What do you know? He even makes her laugh. After Stan leaves she tells me she thinks he's cute. We bond on that, and my dad walks out of the room. He doesn't want to know anything about guys, period.

Stan buys me a pink leather punk-rock bracelet with metal studs, and we kiss for an hour behind the school. It's wonderful. I feel like I have grown a couple of inches in one second.

That night in my room, I write another song. This one is called "My First Kiss." Having a boyfriend really makes me feel like writing songs. Tod and the other guys love my new songs, and suddenly I start singing and playing the bass. Tod's impressed. I'm flying high. All my problems are solved.

Sweetie and Cutie
STORY #4

Everything in my life is going great, if you don't count my brother, Charles, who continues to make fun of my outfits. But I don't care. I have a boyfriend, a band, and cool guy friends, and I'm still managing to get good grades. At my locker at school I pause to soak it all in. I lock my locker up and turn around to see the two toughest skinhead chicks in the school, Sweetie and Cutie, staring at me.

Duh dah ahhhh! HELP! My heart is pounding. Sweetie's arms are the size of boulders. Her legs are like tree trunks. Her boots are immense, possibly twenty-four holes (I don't dare stare too long for fear of getting punched). Her stare is cold. It's rumored around school that she was kicked out of Juvenile because she pulled a knife on a teacher. So they sent her to our public school instead. (Makes me wonder about the public school system, but what do I know? I'm just a teenager.)

Cutie is taller than Sweetie. She has so much mascara on that you cannot see her eyes at all. She looks like a vampire with her white, ghostlike powdered face. On her fingers are tattoos of spiders and knives that spell "knok u out" in black ink. I get a good look at her tattoo as she hangs her scabby long arm around my scrawny neck. If she wanted to, she could easily snap my neck in half.

"Hey, Blondie, what's up?" Cutie asks me.

"*Uh,* nothing," I stammer, melting into the locker behind me as if it were a life vest.

Then Sweetie gets down to my level and stares me straight in my eyes with her murder-on-death-row stare and says, "I see you have been hanging out with Stan. We don't want some trendy little blondie hanging out with him."

Then Cutie adds, "If we see you with him again, you can visit with my two friends."

I come face-to-face with Cutie's fists.

"Got it?" Cutie says with her blood red lipstick smile.

Maybe she is a vampire?

"Got it," I choke out.

I have no rock-ness in me to save myself now.

"Later, Blondie," Sweetie says.

They walk away, laughing all the way down the hall. I watch them and stay against my locker until they are out of sight. Stan turns the opposite corner, comes over and gives me a hug, and says, "What's up, babe?"

"I just had a visit from Sweetie and Cutie," I say tensely.

"Oh, those chicks are crazy," Stan says as he puts his arm around me. "I'm going down to the skate park today. Do you want to come?"

"I can't. I have practice today. But, Stan, they told me if I keep seeing you they are going to beat me up." I feel all bass-player coolness leaving my body.

"They're all talk. Don't sweat it, babe. They won't hurt you. Come on, I'll walk you outside." Stan pulls me in the same direction Sweetie and Cutie walked a few minutes before.

Each step feels like doom. But Stan keeps his arm around my shoulder, so I keep walking forward. We head outside to the front of the school—past the cheerleaders, past the punks. I can see Sweetie and Cutie in the distance. We are approaching them. I can see Tod and the other guys waiting for me. It feels like I will never reach them. I watch Cutie's knuckles from the corner of my eye as we are passing them.

"Hey, Stan," Cutie says sweetly.

Stan gives her the surfer wave.

Sweetie then adds, "Blondie, see you on Monday."

Who's Betty?
STORY #5

All weekend long I dread the thought of going to school on Monday. Everything reminds me of Cutie and Sweetie—TV shows, movies, books, and newspapers. Even my combat boots on the floor look like they are mocking me for my pretend toughness. *I could snap your neck in half, and I am only a pair of boots, ha ha ha!* But no one in my family notices, as this is the big weekend when Charles heads to Brown University.

My parents are leaving me with my aunt Rose for the week. My mom is going through some major mom thing and crying at the drop of a hat. She is constantly hugging and kissing my brother like he's a soldier going off to war. Little do they know *I* am the one who needs them. *I* am the one who might not be here when they return.

All weekend long I have terrible nightmares about being beaten to death. I try to devise a plan of escape from school. The only thing I can come up with is to pretend to be sick. Luckily, on Monday my aunt

Rose falls for the sweaty-palms trick of water splashed on my hands and face. But on Tuesday she informs me, "You look well, but I'll drive you to school so you don't have to ride the bus."

I try to explain on the ride about how I will be severely beaten, maybe even die, if she leaves me at school, because of these girls Sweetie and Cutie.

She laughs. "Come on, Alex, that's ridiculous. They're only teenagers like you, acting out."

Acting out? She wouldn't say that if she met Cutie and Sweetie. She and my mom are such hippies, they don't understand anything about punks and skinheads. She hugs me goodbye and leaves me to my doom, with a happy hippy wave. *She has no idea what I'm about to face. This is not a moment for Zen! This is a moment for panic!* I watch her car leave, swallow the lump in my throat, and run as fast as I can to homeroom.

All week I try never to be alone, especially in the bathrooms. In fact, I hardly go to the bathroom at all. Bathrooms are notorious for being places where bad things happen in school. I make Tod meet me at my locker before practice. After a week he starts getting annoyed, as this cuts in to his flirting time with girls after school. But I was smart to do this, as I have successfully avoided Cutie and Sweetie all week. I'm beginning to think, though, that something strange is going on, because I haven't seen them at all. They seem to have disappeared into thin air.

Stan offers to take Tod's place, and Tod gladly accepts. They both laugh at my expense. And even though I know it's dangerous to be with Stan, I melt in his arms.

"Besides, babe, Sweetie and Cutie got sent back to Juvenile, didn't you hear? They pulled some crap at the school on Monday and got expelled."

I breathe a huge sigh of relief, and then I feel anger rising up inside me. "Why didn't you tell me sooner, Stan?" I say, half mad and half giving in to Stan's cuteness.

"I just thought it was funny how you were reacting, so I kept playing along. I thought it was cute," Stan says with a smile.

Cute? What's cute about genuine terror? I feel so mad at him right now, but at the same time, my relief over discovering that Sweetie and Cutie are gone from my school makes me give him a big hug anyway. He pulls me toward him and says, "Sorry." Of course, I forgive him. I don't want to lose my first boyfriend over something like this.

Stan and I have been dating for one month now, and when I don't have band practice I go watch him skate at the radical (notice, I even have the lingo down) skate park. Stan likes to skate on the ramps. He flies in the air from one ramp to another, effortlessly flipping through the air like an acrobat. Stan hopes to be sponsored someday and go on tour. I think he's good enough to do it (but I'm biased, I guess).

The first time Stan introduces me to some of his friends at the park they all keep talking about a girl named Betty. This goes on for an hour, and I'm getting a bit jealous of this Betty girl Stan seems to know so well. *Is Stan cheating on me?* I panic at the thought. Why does Stan keep talking about Betty? I wish he would stop! I'm getting so angry but have to play it cool, as I do not want to seem psychogirlfriend in front of all these cool skaters. Finally, the guys disperse, skating off to different parts of the park.

29

"Who's Betty?" I finally get to ask Stan. I try to mask my building anger.

He laughs and says, "You. That's what skaters call girlfriends."

"Oh." I feel myself blush. I feel really stupid now, but happy there's no other Betty in Stan's life except me.

During another one of my visits to the park, Stan decides to teach me how to skate. He takes a long time adjusting his kneepads, elbow pads, and helmet to fit me, but now we are ready to go. I feel a little silly, as everything is way too big for me, but Stan guides me to the center of the ramp. All the guys clear the way for me, and I feel like a princess. They all stop to watch and egg me on. Skaters are actually very polite when you are a girl. If you are a boy, they call you things like ass, stupid, and booger and compare how far they can outsnot another guy while skating.

"Go, Betty. Rock on, you can do it," Stan's skater friends shout from the top of the ramp, where they sit as a sweaty pack, holding their skateboards up to their chests. Stan stands next to me and holds me as I step onto his board in the center of the ramp. As I step up, I feel the wobble of the wheels, but Stan keeps his grip around my waist. It feels nice. I look at Stan and smile. He smiles at me. I feel all gushy inside.

The guys interrupt our lovers' lock of a gaze. "Hey, Betty and Stan, move it!"

Stan and I laugh so hard that I almost fall off the board, but Stan catches me.

"All right, babe, bend your knees, and I'll move you," Stan says. "This is called pumping. When you are up high, stretch out. When you are coming down, push down on your knees. Just like this."

Stan pushes me up and down until he is tired and sweaty. This goes on for about half an hour. I feel like I'm getting it, but when Stan lets go of me, I fall on my butt and the board goes flying out into the grass. I look up and see Stan's friends getting impatient. They want to skate.

Stan takes the hint and says, "Let's do this another time. I promise."

He gives me a kiss, and the guys all shout and whistle. I blush and take off all the pads and helmet. Then I climb up to the top of the ramp and watch Stan drop in. He goes right in, and he's off. My guy! *Sigh.*

The Rock Shack
STORY #6

My first night playing music at a real club is at a place called the Rock Shack. Every cool band in town has played there at least once. Tod manages to get The Painted Letters a show because his cousin books the club. You have to be eighteen to get in to the club, but since we are the band they make an exception for us—as long as we stay far away from the bar.

Before I climb into Tod's van my parents give me a long lecture about drinking and being responsible. Having a hippy mom means my mom is supertrusting. But my dad informs me that if I come home drunk, I'm done with playing in bands. This is a good threat for me, as I don't want to go back to my pre-rock-and-roll loser lifestyle! That *would* be punishment for me.

As I walk in to the club carrying my guitar case, I feel like my life is about to change even more. Sometimes I'm afraid it's all a dream and I will wake up and become a loser again at school. But I try to push away those thoughts and just go with it. After all, I'm in a place only people over eighteen go to, because I'm a bass player. Bass-playing has given me access to a world otherwise banned to fourteen-year-old girls.

I take it all in. The long wooden bar scraped and stained with scuff marks and spills. The neon lights advertising "The best beer you can get here." The tacked-up posters of pretty girls with boobs pouring out of tiny bikinis. The band posters plastered on the wall opposite the pretty girls. I notice that all the rock bands seem to be facing the posters of girls—as if they're checking them out. Who could blame them? Even *I* have to stare at the size of the girls' boobs. *Are those for real? It doesn't seem humanly possible, but what do I know? I'm only fourteen.*

There's an old pool table in a corner of the club, and the center of the room is a wide-open dirty slab of concrete that spreads out in front of

a tiny stage framed with Christmas lights. The place smells like bleach, but underneath there's the stench of cigarettes and stale beer. It stinks, but it's rock-and-roll.

Our band goes on first, and the small crowd claps politely after each song. The lights flash on and off, and I get lost in the music. I feel like I'm floating above the crowd. I feel beautiful and cool and tough. Perhaps I'm reaching a moment of true Zen. The sounds float around me on the little stage.

The show is over before I know it, and we remove our equipment from the stage to make way for the next band. I follow the guys backstage to the band room to cool off. Tod sneaks some beers and passes them out to the guys. I drink water.

A guy in a black motorcycle jacket sways into the room after

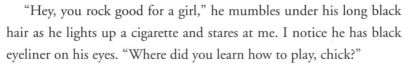

us and plops himself next to me on the bench.

"Hey, you rock good for a girl," he mumbles under his long black hair as he lights up a cigarette and stares at me. I notice he has black eyeliner on his eyes. "Where did you learn how to play, chick?"

"My name's Alex. My brother taught me," I say, a little annoyed at him calling me a chick.

"Yeah, I dig it. But how old are you?" he asks, looking at me with molester eyes.

I pull my skirt down over my knees, feeling uncomfortable. Tod comes to my rescue. He sits down next to me and puts his arm around me.

"She's my girlfriend, man. What do you want?" Tod asks.

I secretly flutter inside, but at the same time I'm amazed that I don't feel like melting. I guess I have gotten over Tod, now that I'm seeing Stan. Tod is my friend. That's kind of cool, too.

"*Eh, eh, eh,* back off, man. I wasn't going to hurt her, just wondering. She looks too young to be that *good* is all," he says, swaying a bit on the bench.

"Thanks," I say. After all, it's a good compliment to get from a guy.

A guy with blue hair pops through the doorway and says, "Chet, what the hell, man? Are you messed up again? It's time to play drums. Hey, guys, sorry, I am Frank. I am playing with Chet in the Rovers, but I see he is not ready to play—*again.*"

We all say hi to Frank and watch as he guides the giant Chet to the door. They don't make it far before . . . and, *blech,* Chet pukes all over the place. The scent of throw-up wafts into the band room and clears everyone out.

Tod sneaks Stan in through the back door and makes a fake stamp on his hand so he won't get kicked out. Then I follow Stan and the guys out into the main room to watch the other bands. Stan is next to me with his arm around me. I stand there and think to myself, *I guess this is what love is like.* Stan talks to me, but the music is so loud I can't hear him. I imagine it's something sweet, and I'm dying to know what he's saying.

"I can't hear you!" I scream, and finally the band ends the song. I smile at Stan, eagerly waiting to hear what sweet words will fall off his wonderful lips.

"I said, I got to whiz," Stan says loudly.

Well, it isn't what I was expecting to hear, but Stan looks so cute I can't help but smile back. He gives me a quick kiss and then leaves my side. I can still feel the touch of his lips making me glow inside. I close my eyes and soak in the atmosphere around me—the loud music, cigarette smoke, flashing lights. I feel giddy.

I sense a presence close by and I open my eyes. Standing there is Cutie.

I want to yell. But no one will hear me above the loud music as the band onstage rips into another song of distorted guitars and screeching. *At least I'm in a public place. People won't allow a fight to break out in a public place, right?* But even surrounded by a roomful of people, Cutie scares me.

"Hey, Blondie," Cutie says, smiling down at me.

I feel my bass-player power waning. I am helpless. I am small.

Cutie towers over me. I can smell beer and cigarettes on her breath, she's standing so close to me. I close my eyes and brace myself for the impact of a punch. I imagine myself being rushed to the hospital in an ambulance. My parents may find me beat to a pulp but I can honestly tell them I wasn't drinking . . .

Just as I sense her hand coming at me I open my eyes and see Stan, my knight in shining armor, placing his arm on Cutie's shoulder—forcing her punch to stop midair like in a karate film.

"Cutie, what's up?" Stan asks, putting his arm around Cutie and guiding her away from me.

He whispers something to Cutie as she walks with him. I'm so relieved, I'm not even jealous that Stan is walking away arm in arm with another girl. I breathe a sigh of relief and sit down at the bar to watch the band—only to get yelled at by the bartender, who tells me to stay the hell away from the bar if I want to stay in the club.

What Guys Talk About
STORY #7

Playing in a band lets me in on what guys talk about. Here are some of the things I hear at band practice:

"Man, did you see Lily at school today? Did you see her boobs?"

"She's hot! I'd do her!"

"I got some new trucks today. Check them out."

"Did you see that video where the guy landed on his head? So cool!"

High-fives always abound, and even I'm included. I'm one of the guys, and they can talk to me about girls and stupid tricks. Before we start band practice, we must watch the latest video of a guy in one of these three scenarios:

Scenario one: A guy nearly gets himself killed, but instead manages to survive the impossible, whether it be amateur boxing, karate, or backyard wrestling. This video is often repeated in slow motion to get the full impact as the guy performing the stupid stunt hurts himself. *Brilliant!*

Scenario two: A guy jumps off an incredibly steep mountain on his snowboard, with an avalanche following him all the way to the bottom.

Scenario three: A guy surfs a fifty-foot wave in a hurricane.

This is what guys dig.

Guys also talk about sex all the time. They think about having sex all the time. Every girl has potential in their eyes. Tod has Jenny, and you would think he would be satisfied. But no, he has a couple of other girls he sees, too. I guess one perfect girl isn't enough. In fact, all the guys in my band are dating several girls at the same time. It makes me wonder, is Stan doing the same thing?

It doesn't take me long to find out. At gym class I make my way around the track and gasp for air after a two-mile run. (Athleticism is not a trait of my family. An hour of meditating and I might have a chance.) I see Stan's face coming into view beneath the bleachers. It happens in slow motion. As I get closer I see he isn't alone. He's with Helena, a cheerleader. They both look stoned. His eyes are red and so are hers. Stan gives me the surfer wave.

I feel tears streaming down my face. I hear my heart pounding inside my head. Like in a cowboy standoff, we're all frozen in our places. Then my stomach takes over, and I run to the bathroom and throw up. I slump down on the dirty tile floor and cry like I have never cried.

For weeks I pine over Stan. I cry more tears than I feel I could possibly have. I never thought that liking someone could also hurt so much.

My solo life never made my heart feel like it was going to break in half. I write lovesick songs, my best one being "You Broke My Heart with a Cheerleader." In fact, you might call this a prolific writing period for me. I fill my diary up with lovesick poems, like this one:

Down deep in the blue

You stole my heart

And tore it in two.

I thought I'd love you till the end of time,

But I was blind, oh so blind.

Meanwhile, at school Stan and Helena walk the halls arm in arm. They seem to be everywhere I am. Stan gives me a wave and a smile, and it is as if we are ships passing in the night, skateboarders rolling past each other. And so ends my relationship with Stan. And so goes a big broken heart.

Never Date Someone in Your Band
STORY #8

I don't have a boyfriend anymore, but I still have a band, and I'm thankful for that. Band practice takes me away from my misery for a couple of hours each day. The only problem with bands is that most guys who play in bands are not too reliable. Everyone doesn't always make it to every practice, so sometimes we have quiet practices to work out new songs. I can count on Andy, our drummer, and Tod showing up on a pretty regular basis, but it's mostly Andy and me.

Andy is fourteen, and unlike the other guys in the band, he doesn't drink. His father is an alcoholic. But Andy does smoke pot. He's always stoned at practice. One of our quiet sessions ends when we run out of things to work on without the other guys around. It's still early, so Andy says, "You feel like killing some time with me? Got a cool spot Tod and I found the other day."

"Sure," I say, and follow him on a hike up through the woods behind our practice space. He disappears around a boulder, and I panic.

Nature makes me nervous. My mind goes straight to horror movies. *Girl alone in the woods . . .* Then Andy reaches out and pulls me up to the top of the boulder. I do my best scream yet.

"Ahhhhh!" Potential Emmy Award–winning scream. Andy looks at me, puzzled. "What was that about?" he asks.

"I'm just a bit uncomfortable in the woods," I say, trying to cover up my momentary weakness with a lame laugh. I sit down next to Andy, trying to act calm, but my heart feels like it is going to explode in my chest.

"This is a pretty cool view, huh?" Andy says, staring out. Then he pulls out a joint and says, "Do you want to get high?"

The joint stares me in the face and asks, *Are you ready for me? No one can resist me . . . You want me . . . You know you do . . . Do you have enough rock-and-roll power to resist me . . .*

I imagine myself puffing up . . . The cloud of smoke drifts away, and I'm a sad, stumbling woman, makeup smeared, hanging in the

gutter, living in a cardboard shack . . . *She could have been something,*
I hear them say . . . *She could have been someone if only she had stayed
away from the pot . . .*

"No!" I shout so loudly that birds fly away from the trees above us.

Andy stares at me, dumbfounded.

"It's cool, no worries," he says.

He smokes his joint solo, and then we start talking about music.
Finally, the atmosphere resumes to normal. But soon we run out of
things to talk about, and a long, uncomfortable silence hangs in the air.
This is the longest time we have spent alone without instruments.

Andy lies down and stares up at the clouds.

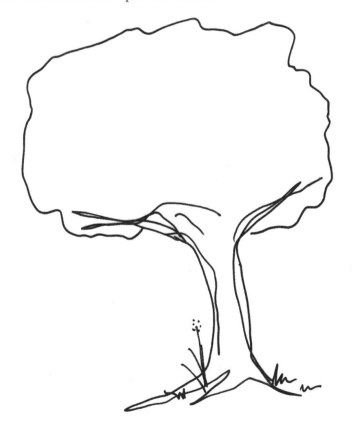

"Check out the clouds, Alex," he says dreamily.

I look up. Just clouds.

"No, you gotta lie down, Alex, watch the world move," Andy says goofily.

I lie down, and we accidentally knock shoulders.

"Now you see what I'm talking about, right?" he says slowly. "I feel like I'm moving, too."

"Yeah," I say. I feel like adding, *And?* I guess it must be the pot allowing him to see something else up there. I concentrate harder, but I feel a headache coming on. Just clouds to me. Then I feel Andy touch my hand. At first I panic. But then I think, well, Andy is kind of cute.

He starts kissing me. Then he says something goofy about good kissing in rhythm and we both start laughing so hard we can't kiss anymore.

"Hey, guys!" Tod's voice interrupts our laughter from below the boulder.

I slide as far away from Andy as I can so Tod won't think anything strange. But Tod doesn't seem to think anything of us being alone together, as I'm one of the guys. He and Andy get high, and then we head down to the practice space to rock out.

Andy and I meet every afternoon at the boulder, in secret, just kissing and talking. He brings picnics and does sweet things like pick flowers for me. He's really funny. He used to be a gymnast and does flips for me on the grass. But one day he starts going up my shirt, and I freak out.

I sit up fast and ask, "Am I your girlfriend?"

Andy lays me back down and says, "Yeah, sure," then resumes kissing me. When he stops for a second, he looks me right in the eyes and says earnestly, "I always dug you, Alex."

And just like that, the girl in me feels special. *I* feel special. I'm Andy's special girl—for three weeks.

I know he's dating only me, since we have band practice almost every day and play three school parties. None of the other guys suspect anything, as far as I can tell. Guys can really be oblivious, as I feel like it's written all over our faces.

After playing one of our greatest sets yet at a big party, I'm feeling especially happy. Not only do I get to rock with my drummer, but we share something even more special. Dare I think . . . *love?* We have great rhythm together is what Andy tells me. I put my bass down in its case and look out to see where Andy is. I see that he's talking to some girl, and a bad feeling starts to smear my love fantasy. I walk over slowly until I catch Andy's eyes. My heart starts pounding.

"Hey, Alex, this is Audrey," Andy says nonchalantly.

"Great guitar playing," she says to me as she smacks her chewing gum and puts her hand on her hip in a cutesy way.

"I play bass," I say stiffly. I feel like adding, *you dummy.* She's blond and very pretty, I notice quickly. I feel my anger rising. *How could I be so stupid? How could I believe Andy would only be with me?* The tension is building. Andy can't look me in the eye. Audrey laughs. It's all so wrong.

"Do you want to get high?" offers Andy.

And I know this is directed to Audrey. I tag along as the kid sister. I am now the third wheel. I watch as they get high and laugh like they are best buddies. They flirt right in front of me. They stare at a lava lamp on the coffee table as they sit next to each other on a couch. They have a "deep conversation" about the lava lamp that only a stoner could appreciate, I guess. To me (not stoned): just a lava lamp.

Then Andy and Audrey disappear, and I'm alone staring at the lava lamp. I feel like throwing the stupid lava lamp across the room. I must have been staring a long time, because Tod comes up to me to tell me the guys are ready to go. To add insult to injury, I have to help load Andy's stupid drums. He has left the party. *Never date someone in your band.*

Over the next couple of months, I have to watch Andy and Audrey together at every show we play, happy as can be. So I enter yet another prolific songwriting period. My favorite song this time is "Stupid Loser Stoner Guy." I get such pleasure from watching Andy bash away at

his kit to that song, *clueless*. But then the joy fades again when Audrey shows up at practice to pick up Andy and they flirt right in front of me. My hurt and pain rise up, and I decide to become straight-edge.

X Marks the Spot
STORY #9

On Saturday afternoons at Old Hundson Church in the industrial part of town there are all-ages shows with straight-edge bands. I go to the shows religiously (ironic for a girl with no real religion other than meditation) and begin my next transformation into Straight-Edge Girl. There's no drinking, smoking, or drug use of any kind, just good punk-rock music. When you walk into the show a person at the door marks you with an X in black marker. X equals crossed arms equals straight-edge.

These are my people. Everyone is here to dig the music. X power fights off peer pressure and going down the bad road . . . into the gutter. I'm X Girl, all pure rock-and-roll power. X power is like putting on a pair of yellow sunglasses that make everything seem brighter.

The Painted Letters play yet another stupid party where my new X eyes cannot take any more drunken teenagers and stoner drummer with girlfriend in tow. I decide I can't be in this band anymore. I confront Tod, who is busy having a smoke with some redheaded girl and flirting.

"Tod, can I talk to you for a second?" I ask.

The redhead glares at me, but my super straight-edge power cares nothing for mean girls. I believe in me! Yeah! X power, go!

"I can't be in the band anymore," I say flatly.

"That's cool. Andy has been teaching Audrey how to play bass, and she's pretty good. She can take your place. No problem," Tod says with a smile, as if this is supposed to make me feel better. Guys do *not* understand how girls think.

Then Tod turns back to the redhead to light her cigarette.

"It's cool, Alex. We'll be fine. She's pretty good, you should see her," he finishes. And just like that Tod has shrunk my X power down to size. *Zap! Where did it go? Some guy can insult me and it's gone? They are replacing me with Audrey?* Now I'm angry—I feel like socking Tod in the stomach—but instead I walk outside to get some fresh air. I feel tears getting ready to flow, but I hear sobbing in front of me that holds them at bay.

It's Jenny. Perfect Jenny is crying? How can this be? I walk over to her and sit down next to her on the curb.

"What's up, Jenny?" I ask, my girl heart opening up like a flower.

Jenny looks up at me, tears streaming out of her perfect pretty blue eyes, and says, "Tod is seeing someone else. Can you believe it, Alex? Why would he do that to me?" I'm speechless, as I know there has been more than one, and another one is inside the house right as we are speaking. So I keep silent and listen.

"I mean, he told me he loved me. He talked about us going to Europe this summer," Jenny continues with a sob.

What a load of crap. Why do we girls believe it all? We are trained at a young age to be the princess and marry the prince. Yeah, right. I feel like telling all six-year-olds what a joke it all is. Throw away your dolls. Don't believe in it! Don't believe the princess crap!

"I'm sorry," is the only thing I can think to say. *I am sorry for all us girls. We are suckers.*

Jenny sobs. "You are so lucky, Alex. You play bass and are cool. All the guys worship you."

What? Guys worship me? *Guys worship* you, *Jenny!* I feel like screaming, but I sit still as Jenny continues.

"All guys see is my outside, but in you they see so much more," she says. I stop to take this all in. My world feels upside down. I never realized being pretty was such a burden. Then I tell Jenny about Andy and me and the Audrey saga, and she starts laughing. There isn't anything like another heartbreak story to bring us girls together. We giggle like best friends. I feel a special bond and perhaps a new power—the power of being a good friend.

The Gospel
STORY #10

I consider asking Jenny to come to one of the straight-edge shows with me to continue our girl bonding session, but then change my mind. Jenny and I shared a moment, but I guess that's all. I mean, we couldn't be more different. The straight-edge kids might scare perfect Jenny. The music she digs is the stuff that gets played on the radio—it's sung by pretty pop stars, not loud, screaming punk-rock dirty musician types. This straight-edge scene is no place for a pretty girl like her— but perfect for the rest of us outsiders, and *me*.

Eddie Monihan, outsider extraordinaire, is the godfather of straight-edge in our town. His band, Five Shades of Light, is the biggest band on the straight-edge scene. They were five skateboarders who decided to rock and stay clean while doing it. Five Shades of Light has their own record label, Stay Right Records, and the band has gone on many tours around the world. They're rock stars, and they do it clean.

Eddie is the complete opposite of all the rock stars who are famous. He does volunteer work for the community and motivates people to do good in the world. His record label donates money to charities, and everyone who works for the record label has to do community service. Instead of using their success for themselves, they spread it around. Eddie is Zen. My mom would like Eddie. He's a hippy at heart, what with all that community stuff and giving—right up her alley.

Since straight-edge shows are always on Saturday afternoons, my parents are okay with me going by myself. Not long after I start going to the shows, I meet a girl named Sal. Sal recognizes me from school and introduces herself. Sal saw me play a few shows with the Painted Letters. She's sixteen and cool. The first time we meet she's wearing skinny plaid pants with safety pins up the side and a cut-up T-shirt with a straight-edge symbol airbrushed on. Part of the straight-edge look is punk, but it's also handmade outfits. All part of the DIY vibe. Sal has blond hair with blue streaks.

Sal is at the show with the guys from her band, All Right. She tells me she's the lead singer and plays a mean guitar. They ask me if I would be interested in playing bass for them. Their bass player just quit. Sal's so nice and cool that I accept without hearing the music. Sal and the guys in her band are all skateboarders, so the first time I meet them for practice it's at the skate park. And, of course, I run into Stan.

"Hey there," Stan says with a smile as he skates over to me. "Coming to skate? I never did give you a good lesson, did I?"

All I can think is, wow, is he actually reflecting? I didn't think guys actually did that—look back on their actions. Then I see Helena hanging out above the ramp, being fawned on by all the skaters. And I feel a hurt deep inside, a big rock in my throat. I feel like I'm going to cry, but I search for my X power and think, *Not here, not now, not in front of Stan. Please hold back the tears.*

Sal skates up to the rescue. It's as if she can hear my X power calling out for help.

"Alex, come over and meet my buds," Sal says as she drags me away from Stan. "Sorry, Stan, *we* need her."

I walk away and feel girl power surging inside me once again as Sal skates beside me slowly, chatting all the way. We leave Stan in the dust. Suddenly, I feel good. Suddenly, I don't care about Stan and Helena.

Sal and the guys ask me if it's okay if they skate a little longer, as they're having a good session, so I sit down next to a group of sweaty skaters who are talking about some guy who skated down the steps of city hall. I roll my eyes but then I am mesmerized by Sal on her skateboard. She's a good skater. She flies across the ramps as well as any of the guys. Sal is way better than Stan. What did I know? I guess what they say is true: Love surely is blind.

A guy named Poppy skates by and gives me a skater hello wave. He's like a Zen master to skaters who come to the park. Poppy is the oldest skater at the park, maybe twenty-seven? At any rate he's a lot older than we are. That's why they call him Poppy, I guess. He has a kid who's five and who's already skating. Poppy used to be sponsored by some skateboard company in California, and then he got really sick and almost died of some rare disease. He lived, but he lost

his sponsorship and then joined the army. I'm surprised he recognizes me. Or maybe as Zen master of the skate park he welcomes everyone the same way. I think my mom and Poppy might get along, too.

There's a division at the skate park, I notice. The stoner kids like Stan and his friends, and the straight-edge kids like Sal and the guys. They don't mix at all. Sal skates up and plops down on the grass next to me, sweaty and exhausted, but with a smile on her face.

"That looks like fun. You're good," I say, hugging my knees.

She crosses her arms straight-edge style and says, "Stay clean, skate mean. It's a blast. You *gotta* try it. I could teach you."

"Stan's my ex-boyfriend. He tried to teach me, but I guess I sucked so much that he gave up," I say.

"You went out with Stan? Sorry, that guy's such a loser. He's cute, but what a stoner loser," Sal says. "You're way cooler than that. And I will teach you to be a better skater than he is. You can show him up. Just you see."

We both start laughing.

Sal's so cool. Hanging out with her is like a high. She's so positive and all about making the vibe good.

"Boyfriends are terrible teachers, anyway. I did much better at skating once I ditched my ex. Straight-edge girls rule!" Sal says, crossing her arms.

I cross my arms, too. I'm glad I met Sal.

"Did you ever feel like smoking pot?" I ask.

"Yeah, but I saw what it did to most of the guys around here. They could have been great skateboarders if they weren't so high all the time. Guess I figured if I practiced hard while they were all getting stoned, I'd get better than them," Sal finishes, looking reflective.

Good mantra. Sal has so much X power, I'm amazed. It all comes from inside her, and she glows with confidence.

"The only drawback to being as good as the guys is that, for some reason, they are afraid to ask me out. I think it kind of confuses them. Paul, my last boyfriend, didn't like that I was a better skater than him. *Guys.* What do I really need a guy for? I got rock-and-roll and skateboarding," Sal continues, leaning back and looking tough. Sal's my new inspiration.

That night I write a new mantra in my diary: *I don't need a guy to make me happy. Happiness is within. If I better myself, I will be strong, just like Sal.*

When I show it to my mom she digs it. She says she can't wait to meet Sal. My mom hugs me and says, "You just might be getting it, Alex."

A Good, Clean Buzz
STORY #11

Before every band practice I meet Sal at the skate park to have a skate-board lesson. Learning to skate makes me feel as powerful as playing in a band does. Gliding along, catching a little air, I feel free of the world. And after a few lessons, Sal even teaches me some tricks. Much like playing music, it's all about getting a good rhythm going. Being a bass player, that comes naturally to me.

"You aren't a Betty anymore, girl. You're a skater. Rad," Sal says, giving me the rock-and-roll fingers in the air.

Even Stan skates over to watch and gives me a compliment. I see Helena glare at me in jealousy. And I feel awesome. I don't *need* a guy. I got the good clean buzz of skaterdom.

All Right starts getting a good buzz, too, around town, and we land an opening slot for Five Shades of Light! My dream come true. I feel like I have just won the lottery. Eddie, the straight-edge godfather himself. My hero, one of my inspirations—and my band will be sharing the stage with him.

During sound check Eddie comes right up to me and says, "I'm Eddie. You guys are in the band All Right?"

I hope my hand is not sweaty as I shake his hand. Eddie knows our band?

He introduces himself to everyone. Even Sal's got a silly grin.

"Sal, I wanted to talk to you guys about doing a record with us. What do you think?" Eddie asks.

I feel like shouting *wahoo!* But I maintain my composure, and I concentrate on setting up my gear. Sal's having a tough time keeping it cool, too, so I look away and pretend I'm busy, to help her.

After Eddie finishes talking to Sal she walks over to me, her face bright red, and says, "Did you hear what he said? Oh. My. God!"

We jump up and down like little girls at a birthday party until the rest of the guys in the band start laughing at us. But I can tell they are excited, too. Guys just don't show it the same way. They try to act even cooler, which can backfire. Chuck, our drummer, accidentally steps into his snare drum and breaks the top of it when he imitates us being girly. Now he has to run to the drum store and get another head, and it's our turn to laugh at him. And John, the other guitar player besides Sal, knocks down a microphone stand while he is imitating us, and he gets a mean look from the sound guy.

Eddie and his band hang out on the side of the stage as we rock the house. The kids love us. We're punk, we're cool, and we're straight-edge. After the show, a guy named Rick, who writes a blog called X Is

In, asks us if he can interview us for his upcoming blog. We all read his blog. He only writes about the best straight-edge bands, some from as far away as England. So right there, all sweaty and stinky, we sit down and do an interview with Rick.

That night I fall asleep with a good clean buzz of thoughts about making a record, doing an interview, and feeling like a rock star. I'm seeing stars. And they're in my eyes.

Can I Help You?
STORY #12

Now that our band is playing more shows, I need to go to the music store every week. Shopping at the music store as a girl is an annoying experience. The first thing the salesman will say to you if you are a girl will most likely be one of the following:

1. Buying a present for your boyfriend?

2. Are you looking for the clothing store down the block? (Like I can't read.)

3. Don't touch anything without asking. This store has breakable items. (Like, am I four or something?)

   Or they say nothing at all. They completely ignore you. As if, if they ignore you, you might just walk out of the store, and then they won't have to deal with you. When Sal and I enter a music store together the music store salesmen really freak out. Not one, but two girls? In their music store? I think women's lib passed them by. My mom would definitely give these guys a hippy talking-to. So, Sal and I do our shopping separately most of the time. Otherwise, it's just too much commotion when you only want to buy some picks and a pack of strings.

When I had to buy a new bass amp I went with Chuck, our drummer, who had to buy some sticks. He breaks them often. This is how it went.

We walk through the glass doors, and are approached by a salesman with supertight jeans that leave nothing to the imagination. (Why do guys think girls dig that?) He has greasy, long, heavy metal hair, a scraggly beard, and a lopsided smile. Overall, a bad look, but what do I know about what adults dig? Sometimes they baffle me.

He addresses Chuck only. "Need any help?"

"Uh, no. But she's looking for a bass amp," Chuck says, pointing to me.

"Oh, really?" the salesman says, pausing. *Impossible* is the word written on his forehead in neon.

"Well, let's go look," he says reluctantly, again only addressing Chuck. It seems to be hard for him to look me in the eyes.

He takes us to the expensive area, clearly thinking girl equals sucker equals dollars. Chuck and I give each other the Look. Then I say, "Actually, I know which one I like." He stares at me like I'm a UFO and I have just landed in his store. *A girl knows what she wants?* I just blew his mind.

"That one," I say as I point to an amp stashed in the corner of the store. I have been eyeing it for a while and am finally able to afford it. It's in the used section, and I can tell the salesman doesn't dig being in this part of the store.

"That one?" he asks, looking stumped. He's frozen in disbelief. Finally, he brings it down and sets it up for me.

"Don't let her touch it yet. I'll go get a bass," he says to Chuck.

Hey, buddy! I feel like screaming, *I'm your customer!* Then he brings out the cheesiest bass imaginable with horns on it and weird flames up and down the body. He sits down, plugs it in, and starts playing. Chuck and I stare in amazement, waiting for him to offer me a chance to play. But he just keeps playing and playing, on and on. Not a great way to make a sale.

Then he pauses, looks up at us, and says, "Pretty good, eh?"

"Well, I can't tell until I try out the amp," I say.

He looks crushed, like a little kid, and I realize he was talking about his bass playing, not the amp. Chuck looks at me and smiles, as if he just got this, too. The salesman shakes it off and then returns to being his cheesy self as he hands me the bass. I sit down and notice as I lean over to change the knobs on the amp that he's looking down my T-shirt. I catch his eye to direct it away, and he smiles a smile that says, *Ooh, you caught me.*

I start playing, and as I reach to adjust the knobs on the amp, his slimy hand touches mine to try to stop me. I instinctively withdraw my hand.

"Hey there, now, I think you gotta have more treble," he says, turning the knobs.

Is this guy for real?

Then Chuck comes to my rescue and says, "This is the way she always plays. We're in a band together, man."

"No way," he says, looking genuinely stunned.

The bass amp is sounding pretty good. I keep playing, giving it a good listen for any crackles, a sign it might die on me on the ride home and leave me short both an amp and my allowance. My mom started giving me more money once Charles went off to school—not sure why. But it allowed me to save enough to buy an amp.

"I'll get it," I say definitively.

As I take the bass and place it on the stand, the salesman says, "Careful, careful, honey."

As we are leaving the store, he hands Chuck a card and says, "You know, she's pretty good. Your band must rock. Let me know if you need an agent. Got a lot of contacts in the music world—big people who can make things happen." He looks impressed with himself. He glances down at my boobs as he says goodbye.

Chuck and I make it to the car with the amp and then burst out laughing.

Being a Girl Rules, and with Two, It Is Cool!

STORY #13

The best things about being in a band with another girl:

1. She understands you, especially when she's as cool as Sal.
2. Unlike guys, she thinks the same way as you.
3. Even though Sal is way into skateboarding, *she* thinks the videos the guys obsess over are stupid, too!
4. She will be your friend forever, no matter what.
5. Unlike with guys, you can count on a girl to be there when you feel low. Guys just tell you to get over it.

Sal and I go thrift store shopping together to find clothes that we can cut up and make into our own cool creations. You have to have a keen eye for pattern and a good imagination for the potential of a piece of clothing to be turned into something cool. Sal is *really* good at this. I'm still learning, but Sal's a good teacher.

So far we each have a couple of cool dresses to wear onstage, some skinny pants, some wild-looking shoes, and many T-shirts. We make headbands out of T-shirts and bracelets out of old vinyl records. Sal and I dye our hair a different color every week. Sal's sixteen, so she's been doing it for a long time and is *really* good at it. Our favorite hair dye to use is called Crazy Hair. It washes out so you can change the color as often as you like. Being girls, our favorite shade is pink, of course. We're punk, but we're still girls—and pink looks good on any girl. It makes you feel cute.

Our number one favorite hangout place is a store called California Girls. Although it was started by two California girls, they aren't blond and cheerleader-like. They're cool. One girl is named Sadie, and the other is Leila. They both surf and skateboard, and they made the shop a place for girls who love those things. They sell everything from trucks for your skateboard to guitar straps, sneakers, hand-silk-screened T-shirts, and their own cool skate clothing line made especially for girls.

On Friday nights they have poetry slams or bands at the store. They do lots of cool things for the community, like plant gardens and donate money to soup kitchens. It's the only store I have ever been in that allows you to hang out as long as you want, even if you don't buy anything. Sal and I have met a whole group of girls at the store who are into the same things we are, and it feels so nice to be in a place where girls support each other. Girl power is definitely a superpower.

Sadie and Leila also let other people sell their creations on consignment, and Sal has some clothing pieces in the shop. Sal's really good at T-shirt designs, and sometimes we skate over to the skate park and think up T-shirt designs instead of skating.

Girl power equals strong women equals true happiness. Sal and I have long discussions with our girl-power friends at the store about things we are going through or have been through with guys. And the coolest thing about everyone there is that they don't rely on guys to make them happy. They're doing cool things to make themselves happy.

Sal and I even make a bet one night to see who can go the longest without seeing a guy at all. The funny thing is, we both lose the bet at the same time when these two cute guys, Sam and Hay, from a band called Seven Stages, ask us both out. And of all places, they track us down at California Girls. After that, we decide we can still have girl power even if we date guys.

I'm in La-la Land
STORY #14

We celebrate Sal's seventeenth birthday at Eddie's studio, Razor Edge, at the same time All Right is recording our first song. Eddie and his friends built the studio themselves in the basement of Eddie's house. I'm amazed that someone who gives so much money away and who never went to college could still have enough money to buy a house. I'm impressed. All paid for by music.

Eddie's girlfriend, Jill, bakes Sal a cake, and she throws an impromptu party in their kitchen when we are done for the night. I wish to be just like Eddie when I grow up. He's the luckiest and coolest guy I have ever met.

I've never been in a real studio before. The Painted Letters always recorded our songs on some crappy equipment in some stoner guy's room. What I'm most amazed at is the amount of equipment—cords, amps, guitars—all gathered in one space. There are black cones on the walls to keep the sounds from bothering the neighbors. The effect is something like a room that is filled with trapped potential: equipment begging to be used, just sitting patiently in a quiet room. The silence seems to be waiting to be filled with something creative. It's surreal. It's like being removed from the world in a time machine made by music.

Recording is like being in a dreamland. Sal calls it La-La Land. Once you put headphones on, nothing exists except the music in your ears. It's wonderful, peaceful, exciting—knowing that a machine is capturing this moment in time forever. That the sounds you are creating might live longer than you are in this world. It's a humbling thought, but it's eye opening at the same time.

Eddie does all the recording himself—all part of his DIY ethic. The mixing room is a small room that has a red leather couch to sit on while you listen to the music coming out of the board and mixing speakers. The first time I hear us back through the speakers I'm amazed. We sound pretty good. Eddie rocks his head as Sal's voice sings out, "Baby, you think you know me, but you don't know, so high and so far below."

Eddie digs us. Eddie digs us! I feel like screaming, but I stay cool. I'm beginning to get good at that.

After one week we finish ten songs, and Eddie tells us he's going to upload it to their website.

And just like that, our music is out there in the world. Anyone any-where in the world will be able to listen to it and buy it if they like it. *Amazing*.

Then something really incredible happens: People start buying our songs. I mean *actually* buying our songs. Eddie thinks we should make a video and put it up, and starts talking about us going on tour. My head feels like it's spinning. We do interviews with fanzines and blogs. I go to shows, and people come up to me and tell me how much they dig our band.

I'm kind of a celebrity. Something I never would have dreamed up for myself. But here I am, a real rock star, and *I* can't even believe it.

My mom warns me not to get carried away. "Remember, fame is fleeting," she says. "Always be *you*."

My mom leaves me a bit in the dark on that one. *Always be me? Who else would I be?* I chalk it up to grown-up hippy talk. I just can't relate.

Bad Things
STORY #15

A band with two girls fronting it gets a lot of attention, because even though there are lots of girls in rock, we still seem to be a novelty—especially to guys. So, every time Sal and I leave the stage, guys corner us. Occasionally they even take it farther than that. Guess I never saw the celebs' side of things when they've gone psycho on the paparazzi. I always wanted guys to want me, but now I think I should be careful what I wish for.

For once, I'm glad I'm not as pretty as Sal, or the lead singer. It gives me slightly fewer problems. *Slightly*. I think about Jenny, and what she said about being pretty. Perhaps this attention is what she was talking about. I guess I'm luckier than Jenny, since this only happens to me at shows. Jenny has to deal with it twenty-four seven. *Good sides and bad sides to everything,* my hippy mom would say to that.

At one of our shows something so bad occurs, though, that I sign up for karate lessons. Sal is in the bathroom changing out of her sweaty show clothes. The guys and I are busy breaking down and loading the gear into the van. The hall is empty except for the bands and a few stragglers. From the corner of my eye I notice a guy hanging out by the bathroom. Our gazes lock for a second, and he gives me such a mean look, my heart starts racing. He turns and walks into the guys' bathroom and disappears. I chalk it up to my vibrant imagination and resume packing. But every time I come back from loading gear into the van, I glance over at the bathroom and notice Sal still hasn't come out.

"What happened to Sal? She too much of a rock star to load her own equipment?" Chuck laughs as he grabs Sal's guitar amp.

"Sal's in the bathroom," I say. "But she is taking a long time."

Then we hear *Bang! Bang! Bang!* from the bathroom door, and Chuck and I run over immediately. The door is locked from the inside, and I have a bad feeling. Chuck kicks with all his might through the cheap door and busts the handle off. The door swings open. Standing in front of us is the guy I had seen earlier. He has his hand over Sal's mouth, and Sal is kicking violently. Her shirt is off.

Chuck jumps into action and leaps on the guy, pulling him down to the floor. They wrestle, but the guy's so big and strong he begins to overpower Chuck. It takes three more people to help Chuck hold him down. Someone else shouts that they are calling the cops. It all happens so fast, my head feels like it's spinning. This is for real.

I run to Sal, throw her shirt over her, and help her out of the bathroom. A big bruise is starting to form across her cheek, and she's sobbing hysterically. Eddie runs over to help, and we walk Sal over to the stage and sit her down. She leans heavily toward Eddie as if she can't support her own weight. She looks sick, like she's going to throw up. As some cops walk through the front doors of the hall, Eddie whispers to her, "I know it is going to be hard, Sal, but you *have* to tell them everything, okay?"

Sal just nods. I rub her back, and Eddie holds her close to him.

The cops come over. Sal has to tell them about the whole awful experience. I feel sick listening to her story. By the end, Sal's shaking and sobbing again, and I'm crying, too. The cops leave, and the three of us sit in silence for what seems like forever, just trying to process what has happened. Things have changed forever. One event. One day. Nothing will ever be the same.

Eddie offers to drive us home. Sal sits in the front seat like a statue. Eddie doesn't say a word as he drives. I sit by myself in the back seat and think, *Why do bad things have to happen to good people like Sal?*

I Am No Kung-Fu Master
STORY #16

Sal refuses to leave her house for weeks. She doesn't feel like hanging out or doing girly things. The band decides to take time off. Sal needs to heal, and we all give her space. She tells me on the phone that she's seeing a therapist, who wrote her a note so that she could take a leave of absence from school. I really begin to miss her when she stops answering my phone calls completely. I feel like it's time for me to pay her back for all the good friend things she has done for me. So I sign us both up for karate lessons. Amazingly, Sal agrees to go with me.

My karate skills, much like my music skills in the beginning, are pretty bad. Sal, on the other hand, is a complete natural. The karate lessons are just the right thing to get her back into this world.

My mom compliments me on what a wise choice I guided my friend to, after what happened to her. *Ah, Confucius says, you are learning, little one.*

The band starts playing again, and we play three sold-out shows in a row. Eddie is always there to look after Sal and me, and he makes sure we are never alone. Sal and I never talk about what happened, and even though she and I get back to our girly routines, I can tell Sal is different. She's more guarded, even around me. We laugh and joke and still do the same things, but it's different.

Then one day at the skate park before practice, Sal and I are lying down on the grass after a good skate session, talking about how much periods suck, and Sal turns to me and says, "That was messed up, huh, what happened?"

I look at her and see some tears in her eyes. I grab her and hold her tight as I can as she cries. We stay like that for a long time.

"I'm sorry," I say. It's all I can think to say. Why do I always draw a blank at these moments? But Sal doesn't seem to mind. She's holding me much tighter than I'm holding her.

Then some skater skates by and says, "Dyke alert! Take it home, chicks," and skates on by.

We both laugh, and Sal says, "Guys are so stupid. We should start spreading a rumor that we are seeing each other. Then we would be protected all the time." She laughs. "But I kind of have a crush on Sil in Halobends. That would kind of ruin my chances with that."

"Hey, I like their drummer, Mick," I say, laughing uncontrollably. "Ooh, double date. Let's ask them out together at their next show. Wouldn't that be funny?"

It's good to see my friend Sal again. She's strong and cool and amazing. She rocks.

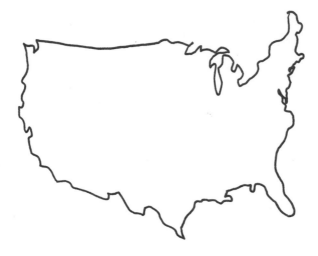

Too Young for Anything That Matters
STORY #17

For three whole months I enjoy the bliss of being a real rock star, playing for hundreds of kids at sold-out shows in and around our town. We even play a couple of shows in New York City. Sal and I can't get enough of New York, and we both vow to move there when we are old enough to get our own apartment. I'm so happy to have Sal back to being herself again and my best friend. I feel like I could be fine anywhere in this world as long as I have Sal in my life.

At my school people recognize me and come up to talk to me about how great my band is. All the outsiders, the punk rockers, and even the skinheads seem to have a newfound respect for my band and me. Eddie sets up a three-week tour that will take us all the way across the country to Los Angeles, San Francisco, and Seattle. I'm beyond excited. I will have to miss a little bit of school, but my parents will understand. I mean, this is amazing!

But the day I tell them, they do not understand. They just say, "No. Absolutely not."

Were my parents abducted by aliens and placed into the bodies of some conservative crazy people?

"Honey, you are fourteen. You can't go on the road with a band. You're just too young. When you're in college like Charles you can do these sorts of things. But no, absolutely no," my mom says.

Where did my hippy, happy-go-lucky mother go? And why does she have to bring up my brother at a time like this? Who are these people? They look like my parents. Damn those aliens. Their replication techniques are so lifelike.

"But, Mom . . ." I start to say.

"No," my mom says, more forcefully this time. "This is not a discussion."

In all the parental talks I have ever had with my mom she has always given me a chance to say my piece. But not this time. No more hippy mantras or good vibes. Just the word no repeated robotically to me.

My life has gone from happiness to tragedy in the blink of an eye. I want to scream like the women in those B movies at some horrific monster coming to attack me—only, it is my parents. I feel helpless, and I'm not allowed to speak.

"We think it's great that you can rock, skate, and have good friends like Sal, who we can tell really care about you, but you're only fourteen. Missing school is *not* okay. Going on tour just isn't something we feel comfortable with, period. You're a child. If you're still interested in this when you are Charles's age, then you can do it."

If I'm still interested? This is it? Don't they see how dedicated I am? How interested I am? Timing is everything. This is my chance, don't they see? How could they do this to me right now? Why would they do this to me?

Then my mom says the most evil thing I have ever heard out of her mouth. "Alex, you must be the big person and quit the band, so if the other guys want to go on tour, they can. That would show maturity on your part."

Okay, so that makes sense. I'm fourteen, a child in their eyes and too young to go on the road. But at the same time I have to be mature? Yeah, that's fair. I feel like stamping like a four-year-old—so I do. *I mean, what else could I do at this moment?*

I feel stuck. So I scream and decide to take my own time-out in my room, away from my alien parents, who have changed into horribly unfair people overnight. It must be some conspiracy.

A week goes by, and I successfully avoid calling the band. But get this, my new, alien mom calls Sal and the guys and forces me, intervention style, to tell them. I hate her right now with all my heart. If she really loved me, why would she make me do this? If she really was a hippy with all that love and goodness, how could she do this to her only daughter?

Aliens definitely abducted my parents, and I must put up a missing persons sign in all the grocery stores. But, then again, no one would believe me. Damn those aliens! They're too smart.

Sal and the guys understand, and they feel bad, but they really want to go on tour, and I don't blame them. They promise to keep in touch, to still be friends.

It is so unfair! Ahhhh! Ahhhh! Ahhhh! My life has been utterly destroyed forever! I will never, ever, ever get over this. Ever.

I scream at my mom, and man if those aliens aren't good impersonators. They use my mom's hippy mantras on me. "This, too, shall pass."

And that just makes me shriek.

For days after, I sulk in my room. I refuse to eat meals with my parents. I go to and from school without saying anything. I'm too upset and angry. And then my mom goes and asks Eddie to come over for dinner so she can talk to him, and I feel like I'm going to die from embarrassment. Why is she trying to ruin everything that's good in my life? She just doesn't understand.

After another week goes by I get kind of tired and bored of being so angry all the time. I finally give up on my crazy alien theory and do "the mature thing" and realize my parents are just being parents. Also, I'm hungry and they have food. Damn them! Man, it would be so much better if they were aliens! I just wish I had someone to get mad at for taking away my happiness in one fell swoop.

The night Eddie is coming over for dinner I beg my mother not to go through with this. I even think about just ditching and avoiding the whole night by going over to Sal's house for dinner. Before I can escape, Eddie shows up early with a plate of nachos he's brought over as an appetizer. My mother is so impressed by Eddie. My parents and Eddie hit it off immediately, and I feel like things can't get any worse, but then my mom starts having a discussion with Eddie the minute we sit down to eat.

"So you see, Eddie, we just can't let Alex go on the road. She's so young. I mean, do you remember how young fourteen is?" My mom looks imploringly at Eddie and grabs my face.

I move my face away and feel like burying it in my plate of spaghetti. Okay, maybe it can get worse.

Eddie smiles and says, "Yeah, that's superyoung. I just forget sometimes when it comes to music, you know? I'm so sorry."

I wonder if this is some conspiracy with people over fourteen to stick together. Eddie has a wonderful time at dinner with my parents. He laughs at my dad's stupid jokes, and my parents are so impressed with Eddie's accomplishments. I just sit and watch and shove as much food down my throat as I can so I don't have to participate in this crazy conversation.

The day the band is set to leave feels like the hardest day *ever*. I see Sal and the guys off as they pack up the van at the practice space. Sal hugs me hard and says, "Keep practicing skating. You better be better than me when I get back."

I don't want to let go of her. I feel like this is the end of my life. I cannot survive without Sal. I never spend a day without her. We both start crying. Not only am I missing the opportunity of a lifetime, but I'm losing my best friend. How could life be so unfair?

As I watch the van turn the corner I sit down on the curb and start sobbing. Just when you think life can't get any worse, it does: Cutie is standing above me.

"Hey, Blondie, what's up?" Cutie says, clenching her fists.

I try to muster up all my X-power toughness. I imagine I'm in a karate film. We dance around each other, preparing for the big fight.

"Nothing," I say, watching her carefully.

I feel like I can't breathe, and I try to stiffen my body and find some inner strength, anything at all. I think of Sal. I think of my band. I think of skating. I think of all my karate lessons. I try to stand tall, but Cutie towers above me. It's useless. She's too tough and too scary, and I feel like releasing more tears. But even they seem to be afraid of Cutie.

"Hey, Blondie, you're in that band All Right, aren't you? You rock," Cutie says. I'm stunned, as if the words have dropped right down out of the sky. *Cutie is complimenting me? Cutie thinks I rock? WHAT?*

"I had you wrong, Blondie. Sorry," Cutie says. "You're going to be big someday, kid."

"I was," I say, forgetting I'm talking to my former school bully. "They just left to go on the road without me."

"*Aww,* that sucks. You were a big part of the sound. Well, I got to run. You should think about starting your own band."

Cutie walks away. Everything seems strange, almost surreal. Then, even stranger, Eddie appears on the street and walks over to me. I feel like I'm in a movie. Eddie sits down next to me and says, "I was looking for you. Alex, I know you are bummed that you didn't get to go on the road because you're too young, but your time will come. Just you wait and see. You got something special." Eddie smiles.

"Yeah, I guess," I say, slumping down.

"When I was fourteen I had a tough time, too. I felt like everyone who was older than me had it so good. My older brother, he was supersmart and great in school, got into Harvard a year early. My parents

82

were so proud of him, and I felt like I would never be able to measure up. How could I ever be a better person than him?" Eddie says.

"But look at all you do now," I say.

"I'm twenty-eight, Alex. It took me a long time to get here to this place. I was pretty lost for a while. I know how that feels. You see people moving ahead and away and doing things you feel like you are missing out on. But you know, when I stopped looking out and started looking within, I started getting to those places I wanted to be." Eddie looks at me with brotherly love in his eyes, and I have to smile a little.

"Keep practicing the bass, learn a new instrument, keep skating, and stay true to where you are and where you can be. It takes a long time—for some people, a lifetime. But if you're focused on where you want to be, you'll be there. I believe it. That thinking is what got me where I am. And who knows what's next? Could be something really different from what I'm doing now, when I up and decide I'm ready for something new. Maybe I'll go to Harvard," Eddie says with a laugh.

"Thanks, Eddie," I say, imagining Eddie with his punk-rock shaved head and tattoos in a preppy outfit.

"I wanted to offer you a job at the label, if your mom says it's okay. Your mom's cool, Alex. You're lucky," Eddie says.

My mom, cool? Not.

"Hey, believe me. My parents never cared about me. My dad kicked me out of the house when I dropped out of high school, 'cause I didn't fit into their mold of the good son," Eddie says.

"Sorry," I say.

"It's okay. I have found a new family now. And lots of good friends. See, when I was growing up, I didn't see that coming. You just never know, Alex. Anyway, I was thinking you could come after school and learn the ropes and all," Eddie says.

"Thanks, Eddie. That's really nice of you to think of me," I say.

"Hey, I enjoy talking to you, Alex. Really, your mom is cool. Some-day you'll see her differently. Let me know what she says. See ya later, pal," Eddie says, rubbing me on the head like I'm a puppy.

Somehow it feels like a brotherly gesture and not belittling. And somehow my sadness lifts, at least momentarily, and I feel a sense of hope again. I run home to tell my mom about Eddie's offer.

A New Direction
STORY #18

My mom and I have a good talk for the first time in a while, and I think about what a great guy Eddie is. My mom agrees to let me work there after school, and she hugs and kisses me and returns to being the hippy mom I know. I guess the alien theory was really whacked, but it was strange there for a while. *I* felt strange there for a while. I'm glad things are back to normal.

For a few months, I go after school to Eddie's recording studio, and although it's an amazing experience, being there's hard, too. All Right is all that everyone talks about there. They've become huge rock stars, and within a couple of months are traveling through Europe and Japan. And I realize that I need to tell Eddie I can't work there anymore. He understands, of course.

In my room, I cry for a while, write in my diary, and then decide to go down to the skate park and practice skating like I promised Sal. At least it would be something to do. I skate into the park, and get a nice hello from Poppy, who is teaching his son how to drop in on the ramp.

No Stan, thank god.

I'm skating along, enjoying the air on my face. It feels good. I get a good rhythm going along from one end to the other. After an hour, I collapse onto the grass, sweaty but energized. Maybe skateboarding is my new path that Eddie was talking about? At any rate, it does make me feel better, and I promise myself to come again as much as I can.

As I am lying there I watch this girl with pink dreadlocks skate around the park. I haven't seen her before. But it has been a while since I've made it down to the park. She skates by me and waves hello. I wave back, and she swings around and stops in front of me.

"Hey, never seen you here before," the pink-haired girl says, wiping sweat off her forehead.

"Yeah, it's been a while. I was in this band, All Right, and we were pretty busy. I haven't had time for skating," I say.

"You were in that band? I thought I recognized you. How come you aren't on the road with them right now? Aren't they in Europe or something? My name's Stella, by the way."

"Alex. Yeah, my parents made me quit 'cause I'm only fourteen, too young to go on the road," I say with a sigh.

"Bummer," Stella says sincerely. "It's good to see a girl around here, at any rate."

"Guy-ville, lately?" I ask.

"Uh-huh," Stella says with a smile.

We both laugh.

"Hey, my friend Molly and I play together sometimes. Do you want to play with us? We are nowhere near as good as you, but we have fun. I'm learning the drums, and she plays guitar. We write our own punk songs."

"Yeah, that sounds like fun, and I'm band-less at the moment," I say, feeling hopeful again. I guess coming down to the park was a good idea after all.

Stella and I chat for a while about music, skating, boys, and school, and I realize that maybe I can move past my recent losses.

Then I look up and see that the sun is setting. I have to skate home. We stay to watch the sky turn rainbowlike and then promise to meet the next day. We skate off in different directions.

I skate down a long hill as the sun sinks into a darkening sky, and I feel like there is nowhere else I'd rather be than right here at this moment with the wind in my face. It feels nice.

Author's Note

When I turned sixteen I decided I wanted to learn how to play the guitar. I definitely didn't know what I was in for when I borrowed my brother's beat-up guitar. The hardest part about learning the instrument was convincing myself that I could do it. When I was growing up there weren't many girls who played guitar, so I was really self-conscious about it. I didn't feel the least bit cool. Instead, I felt like a bumbling giant with clawlike hands that couldn't do anything but make the guitar to go out of tune.

When I finally managed to get the concept of strumming down, I hit my next stumbling block: switching chords. It was a painstaking process, but with a lot of patience and practicing I finally became good enough to start playing in a band.

Now I play bass in my band, Scarce, but I always write my songs on the guitar and love to sit around and sing songs by myself. It's so satisfying and fun. And yes, now I feel pretty cool when I play guitar.

So you want to play guitar too? The first thing you have to do is tell yourself you can do it. *Never* stop saying that to yourself, no matter how awful it feels, and it will feel awful for a while. The second thing you have to do is cut your nails short or you will never be able to get the tip of your fingers down on the guitar the way you need to so the chords ring out just right. You can still be girly and paint your nails all different colors, but you have to have them short.

Learning how to play guitar is really hard when you start, but once you get a handle on a few things you'll be surprised how easy it can be to play. Then you can start a band of your own. Just remember every rock star had to start somewhere, and you can be sure it took a lot of practicing the guitar alone in a bed before he or she became famous. So go out there, get a guitar, and start rocking.

Wondering what kind of guitar you should play? It really doesn't matter what kind of guitar it is as long as it stays in tune. I borrowed guitars when I started, but if you aren't lucky enough to know someone who has one you can borrow, you can look for a guitar at thrift stores, pawnshops, or even yard sales. Who knows—maybe your dad or your aunt has one hidden in a closet, just waiting for you to claim it for your own. Remember, one man's trash is another girl's treasure. Also, it's helpful to have someone who knows how to play guitar to help you find one that stays in tune.

With an electric guitar, you need an amplifier to plug into. The best kind to start with, especially while you are practicing your chops alone, is a practice amp. Practice amps are small, quiet (you won't disturb the parents), light (take it anywhere), and sound pretty decent. They're simple and easy to use: just plug it in and turn it on. You can use headphones with it if you really want to rock out and make some noise.

THE GUITAR AND ITS PARTS

So now that you're a proud guitar owner (or borrower), it's time to get to know your guitar a bit better. Here's a picture of a guitar with all the parts and what they do. Pretty soon, you will be Miss Rocker and these things will slip out mid-conversation with people, and they'll look at you like you are from another planet. It's so fun!

Just like us girls, guitars come in all shapes, sizes, and colors. Each guitar can be special in its own way. Have fun finding one that fits the kind of girl you are and treasure it like it's your best pal, because at times it can get you through things just like a good friend.

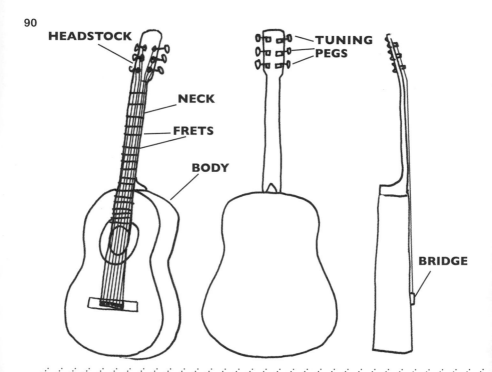

BODY—The main part of the guitar where you strum the strings.

NECK—Where you play your notes and chords (and later on your rip-roaring solos).

HEADSTOCK—Where you do all your tuning.

PICKUP—Electronic device that is a magnet wrapped with wires to catch the sounds from the metal strings. (If your guitar is really nice, it will have two of them; then you get two sounds to choose from.)

VOLUME KNOB—A knob adjusted to make the sound come out louder or softer.

TONE KNOB—A knob adjusted to make the sound of the guitar change from bright and high to low and deep or somewhere in between (depending on what sound you prefer).

TUNING MACHINES—These either tighten or loosen the strings of your guitar depending on which way you turn them.

TUNING PEGS—These guys work hand in hand with the tuning machines—the strings are wrapped around the pegs, so when you turn the machines they spin the pegs around to tighten or loosen the string.

BRIDGE—Holds the bottom of the strings in place.

GUITAR JACK—Where you place the guitar cord to connect the instrument to the amplifier (on some guitars it may be on the bottom).

STRAP PIN—You put your guitar strap around these two pins so you can stand and rock!

FRET—thin metal bars that you press the strings against to make a note or a chord.

STRINGS—(From top of the guitar to the bottom) Low E, A, D, G, B, High E.

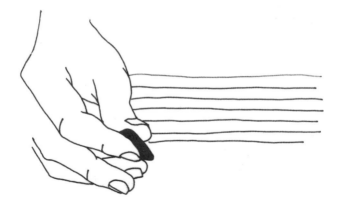

HOW TO STRUM A GUITAR

Before you even try playing chords, it's a good idea to practice strumming the guitar. You will probably feel pretty stiff and awkward when you try to strum at first. But you want to be loose and relaxed. You hold your pick between your thumb and index finger. Move your hand up and down, using your wrist. The pick should hit the string at a ninety-degree angle. It always helped me to imagine I was a rock star I worshiped when I was practicing my strumming. Sometimes just getting into a good pose will help loosen you up.

As you get better and more relaxed, you can add more of your arm into the motion. Then you can really rock! And remember to make lots of mistakes and awful noises (that is part of the learning process). You've got to do that before you can be strumming the guitar like your idols. They did the same thing, so don't feel silly and just let your inner rock rule.

A COUPLE OF CHORDS ON THE GUITAR

Four of my favorite chords are E major, A major, C major, and G major. I found it easier to look at someone doing the chord than reading the notes sometimes, so I included some illustrations of the chords. If you place the pictures in front of you and look really carefully and place every finger slowly in its correct place, you will make the chord. I marked an X when the string shouldn't be played. All of the hand positions are done with your left hand. You strum with your right.

Here's where the short nails come in handy. The key to getting the chord to ring out nicely is getting the tip of your finger (that would be hidden under long nails) to press down on the string. It has to be the very tip of the finger or the string will buzz. You will get big marks in your fingers at first, as you'll have to press really hard to get the strings to ring out. This will hurt a little. But soon those marks will turn into calluses and it won't hurt a bit. And don't worry—no boys ever noticed my calluses. If they did, they thought it was super cool that I had them, especially once they saw me rock out on the guitar.

The other important thing to remember when playing chords is to make sure that you position your finger between the two metal bars (frets). If you touch the bars the chord will sound like a buzz. Last thing to know is what your thumb is doing mysteriously behind the neck of the guitar. The flat part of your thumb should be about halfway between the top and bottom of the back side of the neck of the guitar. Just remember, be patient, and have fun.

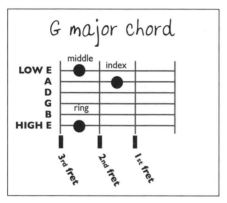

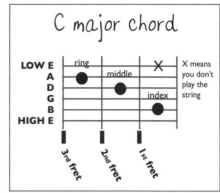

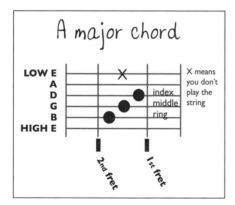

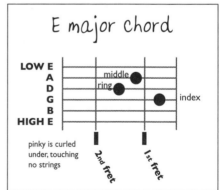

● **where YOUR fingertips are**

WRITING SONG LYRICS

I always kept a diary growing up to write down poetry and song ideas or to draw. If you want to write songs I would advise getting a diary or a notebook and take it with you wherever you go. You never know when inspiration will strike. It really helped me a lot when I was sad and had no place to put that sadness. It got me through a lot of bumps and bruises. What's cool is that you end up with something positive out of that sadness. You create something magical and special—a song. Here are the lyrics to a few of my songs I wrote with Scarce to get you started and to see how easy it is. You can listen to any of the songs on iTunes if you want to sing along.

This is a song called "Hope." I wrote it about a boy and then he dumped me, but I still got a good song out of it. *Hope* it inspires you to write (hee hee hee!).

Hope

Lay your head across my lap
Think of all the things you said
You told me that everything's not tainted black
You told me, you told me,
You told me to look inside
You told me, you told me,
You give me hope to carry on
You give me hope to carry on

Oh, oh, oh, oh, oh
You put stars in my eyes
Oh, oh, oh, oh, oh
Like some big, big surprise

Hold your hand up to my heart
Listen close, listen close,
Before we met it fell apart
Listen close, listen close,
You said look at that thing on your shoulder
Let me hear it sing
Let me hear, let me hear it sing
You give me hope to carry on

Oh, oh, oh, oh, oh
You put stars in my eyes
Oh, oh, oh, oh, oh
Like some big, big surprise
Oh, oh, oh, oh, ohhhhhhhhh (let it ring out, baby!)

I wrote this song about a friend who had gone out of my life for a while. I missed my friend and was really sad about our parting of ways. This song helped me get through the split and even rekindled our friendship. My friend thought the song was so sweet. It healed a lot of bad wounds. Songs can be magical that way.

The Long Goodbye

It was a broken heart
That you wanted to jumpstart
It was a sunken dream
Floating backwards in between
It was a long goodbye
In the middle of the night
It was a long goodbye
In the middle of the night

How could I know that
I would miss you
How could I know that
I would miss you

Staring up to the sky
A firecracker in your hands
And I did not even know
We were coming to the end
So it was a long goodbye
In the middle of the night
It was a long goodbye
In the middle of the night

How could I know that
I would miss you
How could I know that
I would miss you

Here is a song called "Ocean Blue" that I wrote about when I was so depressed that I couldn't do anything but cry.

Ocean Blue

Look at how far we've sunk
I'm feeling along the bumps
I'd like to float down with you
All the way down to this blue
In this ocean blue
Ocean blue

Take me down, all the way down
'Cause I wanna be with you
Take me down, all the way down
'Cause I wanna be with you
I want ocean blue

And where have you gone
Well, my angel sang me pretty songs
And there's just a ghost of you
Underwater I can see
Through this blue
And wave after wave of your hand

I'm kneeling down
I'm at your command
In this ocean blue
Ocean blue

Take me down, all the way down
'Cause I wanna be with you
Take me down, all the way down
'Cause I wanna be with you
I want ocean blue

Okay, now that I've laid my words out to you and bared my soul, it's your turn to get started writing.

103

GO OUT AND ROCK!

I hope using this book will get you started playing. I tried to keep things as simple as possible. That's the way I got started. Be patient—it may take you a while. I remember sitting in front of my practice amp in my room, playing the same chords over and over, and over again, thinking, *This will never come to me.* Switching between chords seemed to take me forever, and my fingers would be in so much pain, I just cried. Then all of a sudden one day, it just happened, and I started strumming and changing chords easily. It was the most wonderful feeling!

One of the best ways to get comfortable on the guitar is learning your favorite songs. If you know how a song is supposed to sound, you know when you are doing it right or wrong. The other thing to do is to get your girlfriends to learn with you. It's always more fun learning something when someone else is, too. You still have to practice by yourself, but it's nice to have some company when you feel like you're having a hard time. Who knows—maybe you can start your own band. When I wanted to learn how to play drums and some of my girlfriends wanted to learn how to play guitar, we decided we would do it together as a band. We had so much fun! We even played a show!

I hope this book will get you into playing guitar, and then you can take some lessons, and then go out there and rock! Then again, the greatest thing about playing guitar is that it's just as much fun playing by yourself in your room. Rock on and have fun!

JOYCE RASKIN grew up in the inner city of Washington, D.C., being exposed to music, art, and other forms of culture. She attended one of the few bilingual elementary schools in the country at the time, where she became fluent in Spanish. The influence of her grandmother, who was a painter and sculptor, mixed with this exposure to other cultures, led her to pursue her education in the field of art at the Rhode Island School of Design. She graduated in 1994 with a BFA in illustration.

While finishing her degree, she began playing bass guitar in a band called Scarce. Shortly after her graduation from RISD, Scarce was in the throes of a major label bidding war. After choosing to sign with A&M Records, the band toured Europe, England, Canada, and the United States. Things seemed destined to take off, but shortly before their debut record was due to be released worldwide, Scarce's lead singer suffered a brain hemorrhage and was in a coma for eighteen days. Miraculously, he survived and was able to play music, but the strain of the illness took its toll on the band, and members of Scarce parted ways for several years.

Joyce then went on to begin a career as a children's book designer in New York, working for Simon and Schuster and then Scholastic. She relocated to Massachusetts in 2004, where she began working as a packaging designer. In 2008, Joyce released her rock-and-roll memoir entitled *Aching to Be* on Number One Fan Press. Joyce Raskin's book about the band's experience led Scarce to re-form and play their first sold-out show in eleven years in Boston in the fall of 2007. Since then they have toured the UK and Scotland to promote the release of Sally Irvine's documentary about the band, called *Days Like These.*

Tattoos and Parades, Scarce's first reunion recording, was released in October of 2008; highlights include the melodically surrealistic pop waltz "Imagining It" and "Dust," a moving and jarring eulogy to their friend the highly regarded guitarist/songwriter Chris Whitely. In addition to working on a new album of their own recordings, Scarce has been working on a set of children's songs for Curious George. *Curious Baby Curious George Nursery Songs* and a full-length Christmas album entitled *Curious George Christmas Carols* will be released in 2010. On these sessions they explored using acoustic guitar, piano, slide guitar, and harmonica and bringing more of a country feel to their sound. Look out for Scarce in a city near you.

Albums by the band Scarce:
Deadsexy
Girl Through Me
The Red Sessions
Tattoos and Parades

Joyce currently lives with her family in Boston, Massachusetts. You can e-mail her or the band at scarcetheband@gmail.com. For free music downloads, videos, and the latest news on the band, visit Scarce on Facebook at www.facebook.com/teenrockstar.

CAROL CHU hails originally from Tennessee. She has a degree in journalism and a master's in design and has worked as a reporter and designer. Her work has been featured in various publications and design competitions, and it is also in the permanent collection of the Library of Congress.

When not busy with design, she lectures on typography and visual systems. She's worked at design studios, fashion magazines, and publishing companies.

Currently, Carol is an art director and designs books of all sorts (always while wearing her headphones!). She spent many happy evenings at the Black Cat and the 9:30 in Washington, D.C., bopping around.

Rock Star
Acknowledgments

I'd like to especially thank Julia Richardson for being such an excellent editor and guiding me through this adventure of my first novel for teens. You rock. I'd like to thank Betsy Groban for giving me this opportunity to share my rock-and-roll book with teenagers everywhere. So happy to have the most rocking designer, Carol Chu, to design and illustrate my book. Thanks to Sheila Smallwood for giving me the gift of working with Carol. Thanks to Mary Wilcox and Monica Perez, who have encouraged me and continue to support my rock-and-roll endeavors in so many ways. Thanks to Karen Walsh, Jenn Taber, Julie Bartynski, Emily Meyer, Cynthia Platt, Donna McCarthy, and Margaret Melvin, who have shared their enthusiasm and support with me. Thanks to everyone at Houghton Mifflin Harcourt for giving this rock-and-roll girl a chance to shine. Thanks to my parents, whom I love so dearly and whom I cannot ever thank enough for making me feel like the world is my oyster. Thanks to my brother, Steven, for teaching me to play bass, and to Miss Johnna M. for being a sister in rock. Thanks to Owen and Nancy White for being a surrogate family. Thanks to Eva Black for love and support. Thanks to my husband, Matt, and my children, Syd and Lizzie, whom I love with all my heart. Thanks to Exene Cervenka whom inspired me to rock when I was a teenager and kindly lent her warm words of encouragement and support for my book. Thanks to Mary Timony my fellow rock-and-roll teenage rock star in arms. Thanks to all supporters of my rock band, Scarce. Thanks to everyone who reads this book. Rock on. Pick up an instrument today and start making some rock in your life.

Joyce